TRINITOGA

stories of life
in a
roughed*up
tough*love
no*good
hood

BY the authors of Beacon House:

Trinity Alston, Reiyanna Davis,
Jonae Haynesworth, Serenity Summers,
Temil Whipple, and Zoe Williams

SHOUT MOUSE
PRESS

In collaboration with Shootback and
Shout Mouse Press

Published by
Shout Mouse Press, Inc.
www.shoutmousepress.org

Copyright © 2014 Shout Mouse Press, Inc.
ISBN-13: 978-0692266335 (Shout Mouse Press, Inc.)
ISBN-10: 069226633X

All photography produced in partnership with Shootback Project
Cover and interior cover photographs by Jahmes Hamilton
Interior photographs:
Reiyanna Davis (p. vi, 23), Jahmes Hamilton (p. 7, 18, 23, 27, 44),
Jonae Haynesworth (p. 12, 15), Serenity Summers (p. 2, 15, 32), Zoe
Williams (p. iv, 37)

This book is for all the kids
who have had bad experiences,
like when they don't realize
how much
they need someone
until they're gone.

prologue

We started with Setting. "Trinitoga" was born from the melding of names of two nearby neighborhoods—Trinidad and Saratoga—and its original description was powerful, gritty: "Rats everywhere, trash everywhere, a street at the end where they sell drugs, called 'The Strip.'"

We quickly moved on to Character. Who lives here? Who rules this place, and who hates it? That particular day when we were brainstorming there was rumor of a guy with a gun outside the safe confines of Beacon House, so we put him in the story. "Call him Shoota," the authors said. "Give him anger issues, and a fade."

We met everyone else after that: Baquisha, the mother of Shoota's teenage children, and then the kids themselves: Rude Boy, Rude Girl, and Tianna. We met their friends and their boyfriends and girlfriends and their grandmas. We learned what made each individual unique. What made them happy. What made them scared. How they were connected. How they weren't.

And then we started writing.

Trinitoga is a novel-in-stories. Each writer selected a character from our list and then told the story of some powerful moment in that character's life. Some of those stories intersect or overlap. There are flash-forwards and flashbacks. You'll see a moment from one character's point of view and then the same moment from another's. They'll see things differently. That's one of the reasons this form is so successful and so true-to-life: it's messy. There is no one "truth." There are many different experiences of reality, and sometimes people live truths inside themselves that others do not see. Rude Girl, we learn, is not only rude. Sharkisha is not only a thug. Baquisha, for all her faults, had higher hopes for herself and for her children, too. And Shoota—the character who started it all and causes so much destruction to his family—we meet first as an innocent, sweet, scared little boy who makes a mistake and is forever changed. Those who only know him as an adult have no idea.

The level of complexity in these characters and in their relationships with one another is a testament to the insight of these writers. They see things. They say it like it is. They put hard truths in sharp relief: "She felt sad on the inside, and angry on the outside." Reading these stories is a way to appreciate and understand the ways the writers themselves are making sense of this world. As one writer says in her bio, "Writing this story was a way of telling people what is going on in my life without people knowing some things are really me."

There is a lot of drama in this book. A lot of violence, a lot of anger. There are multiple trips to the hospital, and for multiple reasons: gunshots, getting beaten, overdosing. The repetition is powerful—it immerses us in a world where this sort of overwhelming and uncontrolled trauma is not only possible, it is happening. This is what life feels like for these characters: swift and sudden changes in emotion, swift and sudden acts of violence. It's the stuff of high drama, certainly, but there is emotional and empathetic truth driving this struggle. Writing fiction gives us a chance to imagine everything happening at once, without restrictions, to put ourselves in the worst possible positions, and then to write our way out. It's a way to take control of the story, and in fact to take control of our own stories, too.

✹

A note about editing and language:

These writers did a tremendous job putting their voices on the page. They wrote in a variety of ways: typing on their own, editing with a story coach, dictating, revising solo. These stories are their own. During the editorial process, due to the nature of the project—multiple stories written by multiple authors over multiple weeks with multiple plotlines—we occasionally had to create bridges and connect dots. In all cases we aimed to maintain the consistency of authors' wishes and authors' voices.

Also, we treat writers like writers, like artists. Their highest charge is to be authentic, to be genuine to the situation and to the characters at hand. Thus in fraught emotional conflicts, characters may use emotional language. We ask writers to take this responsibility seriously—to evaluate the effectiveness and necessity of all choices, and to recognize impacts on audience—and we are proud of their thoughtful consideration of these issues. Please be advised that because we do not censor the experiences or imaginations of our authors, this book may contain adult themes and language.

It was a privilege to write with these authors. These stories, these characters, and these voices have stuck with me. I learned much from these writers on our spring Friday afternoons, not only about fantastically good dialogue (!), but also about the courage to explore both the unknown and the (quietly) known, in-depth and with heart. Enjoy the wild ride ahead of you, and appreciate these talented voices on the page.

-- Kathy Crutcher
Founder, Shout Mouse Press

photo by Zoe Williams

Trinitoga is where
we all grew up,
and everyone's a big family.
It's a roughed ✳up hood,
but we all got tough love
for each other.

trinitoga

Take a step outside and look. You'll see trash, you'll see smoking, you'll see drug dealing, fighting, and killing. A lot of people live there, like a whole bunch of Vienna sausages in a square can. Some people are bad, but some are good. Half and half. The bad people get in trouble all the time, smoking and drinking and messing around. The good people stay in the house and tell on people who are doing bad. People are getting robbed for shoes, getting their bikes stolen. Everybody's not from the same hood, but they're all real close, so if they see you fighting or getting jumped, they'll step in.

There are lots of apartment buildings in Trinitoga. They're brick on the outside and brick on the inside, too. They have hardwood floors, but half the doors are bleached. Everybody throws bleach at the doors of the people they don't like because the bleach stains, and then the doors have white spots on them. The city built a new playground, but the kids broke it up on the first day. They threw rocks and glass at it and were smoking and drinking in the playground.

If you move here and you see what it looks like, the boys are going to jump you to test you out. You pass by fighting back.

This is where we all grew up, and everyone's a big family. It's a roughed-up hood, but we all got tough love for each other.

map

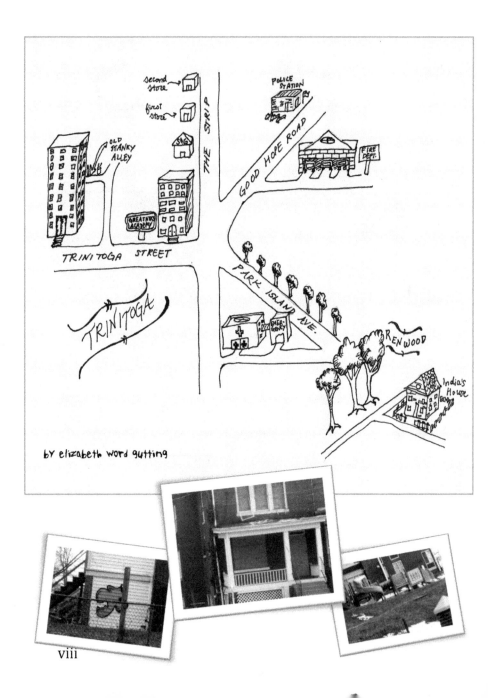

by elizabeth word gutting

characters

Shoota is the father of Rude Boy and twins Rude Girl and Tianna. He's the long-time on-and-off-again boyfriend of Baquisha. Shoota is the King of the Hood, with anger issues and a fade. He always carries a gun on his hip. The smallest noise sets him off. Once, he was a good kid, back when he was still Chris, before he became Shoota.

✻ story by Serenity Summers

Baquisha is the mother of Rude Boy and twins Rude Girl and Tianna. She's the long-time on-and-off-again girlfriend of Shoota. Baquisha "puts the get in ghetto." She's a drug addict, and she tells her kids to do the right thing, but she doesn't set a good example. Again and again, Baquisha tries and fails to be who she wants to be.

✻ story by Reiyanna Davis

Rude Boy is the oldest. He's following in his father's footsteps, selling drugs, and thinks of himself as the Prince of the Hood. He loves his dad and idolizes him, even if his father is a bad dude. Rude Boy is bony and thin but tough. He wears saggy clothes. People are scared to stand up to him.

✻ photos by Serenity and Jonae

characters

Sharkisha is Rude Boy's girlfriend. She fights a lot and has a special punch and a song that she sings when she's in a fighting mood. She and Rude Boy are tight, though. They have a great bond and depend on each other. Sharkisha wears her hair in tracks and they're falling out. She's embarrassed by her mother.

✳ story by Temil Whipple

Rude Girl is rude. She talks over people and has an attitude. She doesn't get along with her twin sister, Tianna, or with her older brother, Rude Boy, either. She doesn't get along with anyone. She's sad and angry with her mom. Rude Girl wears her hair in a bun and carries around a cracked phone. She keeps a lot inside, so on the outside she's—you guessed it—rude.

✳ story by Zoe Williams

Tianna is Rude Girl's twin, but she is her exact opposite. Tianna is nice. She is smart and kind and wants out of her angry family. That's why she's best friends with India. She loves India and India's grandmother and spends all her time with them, where everything is easy. She wants to run away. She wants to get out of Trinitoga. For good.

✳ story by Jonae Haynesworth

characters

India is Tianna's best friend. She's nice. She has long hair and
light skin, and she wears braces and sometimes glasses, too.
She's shy until you get to know her, and then she's a firecracker.
India lives with her grandmother in a nicer neighborhood
nearby called Renwood. Tianna goes to India's house all the
time to get away from her family.

✹ story by Trinity Alston

india's grandma (gmama)

India's grandma is much nicer than other adults. She doesn't
yell at children, and she doesn't carry a gun. Unlike other adults,
she sets a good example. She's got a good job as a librarian at a
nearby library and treats both India and Tianna like they are her
own. Gmama wasn't nice to her own daughter, India's mother,
and then her daughter died when India was very young. India
thinks her parents were in a car accident because that's easier,
but really her father is in jail for life because he was a bad guy.
He made her mother so sad she died of heart cancer. When you
grieve for a long time, that's what happens: you get heart cancer.
So now she's gone, and Gmama understands that life is short.
Now Gmama is nice to everyone. She is a very old lady and only
has a little bit of life left, so she wants to live it right.

✹ characterstorm by Tyona Calloway

Chitty
Chitty
Bang
Bang

ʃʰooₜₐ

This is the tale of Shoota. His real name is Chris. He grew up in a really bad hood called Trinitoga where everyone was killed by guns. BANG BANG POW was all you heard.

Chris was a nice boy. Always quiet. He used to stay in the house all day, playing with his toys and watching TV. Then, one day, everything changed.

It was a Sunday afternoon in the summer. It was hot and everybody was outside chilling and talking. Chris was sitting in the house waiting for his parents to come back from the grocery store.

Suddenly he heard gun noises. They sounded like BANG BANG POW. He hurried to the window and looked out to see what was happening.

On the porch, he saw two bodies. He didn't know who they were at first until he looked more closely. Then he saw his father's Jordans and his mother's curly long hair. They were face down. He was confused. He ran outside to help and saw a pool of blood spreading thick and dark on their backs.

After that, Chris had to live with his grandma, who lived two doors down. He and his grandma were best friends. They went everywhere together. They went to the movies and to the skating rink. The love was real.

But then his grandma got very sick. He got worried because he was having a good time. He didn't want all of the fun to stop.

When he went to school, he made a good friend named Baquisha. They always talked to each other. They always talked in the back stairwell. They always passed notes in class. He realized that she was just like him, living with her grandma, too. They both were really worried because both of their grandmas were sick.

One winter day in the afternoon, Chris went home. The house was very quiet. Too quiet. Chris's heart started to pound. He rounded a corner and found his grandma on the floor. She was not breathing. He shook her to see if she was OK, but she was not breathing, and she didn't blink, and she didn't answer when he said "Grandma."

He hurried and called the ambulance. They came as fast as they could. They came in ten minutes. On his knees, Chris was crying and screaming and shouting. None of it helped. He knew that she was gone.

✵

The next day, Chris went to school sad. He told the teacher what had happened.

He said, "My parents got shot, and my grandma died, and I have nowhere to go."

"You can live with me," Baquisha said. "My grandmother's too sick so I'm back with my mother, and I hate her, but at least it's a place to stay."

Chris had no other choice, so he said yes. He was grateful to have a friend.

They lived in a house two blocks away from Chris's old house. Baquisha's mother let Chris live with them because he had nowhere else to go. They had to do a lot of chores and really couldn't go anywhere but school. Chris was treated the same as Baquisha—they always got in trouble for doing nothing. So Chris started spending more time outside to get away from Baquisha's mother.

Chris began to embrace the streets. He was angry because he had no one to love him and take care of him. Now little nine-year-old Chris was no longer a good boy. He was changed forever.

❋

One day Chris found a gun outside in a crack in a wall. The gun made him feel like he had a lot of power. He had never held a gun before. It was cold and it was light. He wondered: *Is this the gun that shot my parents?*

He went and told his best friend Mike.

Mike was scared that Chris might go to jail. He said, "Chris, you better put it back, because I'll tell the police that you have a gun and you'll go to jail." Mike had seen a lot of people get shot before and go to jail.

Chris said, "Shut up before I shoot you." The gun had an effect on him. The gun made him feel like he was on top of the world and could do anything. He pointed the gun at Mike. He was very scared, and he didn't really want to do it.

Mike begged for his mercy. He said, "No, please, I'm sorry."

Chris lowered the gun. He was never really going to shoot him. But then his finger slipped on the trigger, and he shot Mike in the stomach.

Mike instantly fell, and blood rushed out from his side. His eyes were open and he was traumatized. He couldn't move.

Chris started to cry. He stared at his friend and tried to figure out how to save him. But by the time he was about to get

5

him out the door, Mike's eyes closed, and Chris couldn't feel him breathing anymore. Mike's body got lighter because a lot of blood ran out.

Chris felt bad. He couldn't think straight. He wanted to run away. But first he wanted to figure out where to hide the body. He thought if he couldn't hide the body he was going to go to jail for life.

Chris ended up hiding his friend in an alley behind a trashcan. He started crying even more. Mike looked like he was sleeping. Chris remembered him and Mike being friends since they had been born. They used to go on family outings with each other and play with cars. Now Mike was gone.

This hardened Chris. He had been through too much too soon. He remembered once again that not everybody was going to be there all his life. He felt pain, but he also felt like anyone who disrespected him was going to get killed. That was the only way to survive. He had nobody to take care of him now, so he had to do everything on his own.

After that, Chris didn't really care about what anybody thought. He had no problem killing people. He killed some people from his neighborhood because they asked him a lot of questions and he got irritated. He killed people who tried to play jokes on him. He killed people who tried to be his friend but always talked about him behind his back.

Soon everyone was scared of him. Many people were scared to tell the cops. All the people of Trinitoga wanted to be his friend.

At the age of 15, Chris changed his name to Shoota. He never looked back.

 by Serenity Summers

This hardened Chris.
He remembered once again that
not everybody was going to be there
all his life.
He had nobody to take care of him now,
so he had to do everything
on his own.

baquisha

Once upon a time, there was a girl named Baquisha, and she came from Trinitoga. Baquisha wasn't exactly the brightest girl when she was little. She actually was in a Special Ed group when she was in school. She had trouble focusing, so she got really frustrated at different people when she thought they were trying to get on her nerves. Other kids made fun of her because of her attention span. Other kids said, "Are you dyslexic?" She took those comments as threats and she said, "No, I'm not." All her life, people picked on her because of her condition.

She had a rough life at home, too. After her grandma died, she lived with her mom and her aunt, and sometimes her dad visited. But they got kicked out because her mother didn't clean up, their house was atrocious, and they didn't pay rent. Baquisha felt like her mother didn't really care about her.

So, in her lifetime, she didn't become very successful because she got frustrated all the time. When she had jobs, her bosses always said things to her like, *To be successful you have to be able to listen to people, and take criticism.* But she said that she couldn't, so her bosses sadly had to fire her from all of those jobs.

Finally Baquisha got a job at a placed called HEX. HEX was a packaging deal center that took heavy packages, the ones the post office thought were too heavy and that might have something inappropriate inside them. Hex would take anything if they got paid for it. Baquisha had decided that was a good job for her, and she actually was working very well until a man named Jerome started working there. He brought back memories from Baquisha's mother and how she treated Baquisha unfairly sometimes when she was a child.

One day Jerome asked her to go put the boxes on top of the shelf, and she said that her ankle had twisted the day before, so she couldn't work that day. So Jerome asked her why she was even there, if she couldn't work. Baquisha said she was just there so she could get free money, for her paycheck, and for her kids, or else she was gonna have to get some food stamps.

"Well if you want your pay, you have to work. I'm gonna tell the boss you haven't been working and unless you want me not to, you need to put the boxes on top of the big shelf."

So Baquisha responded by yelling at him and doing inappropriate things with her finger, plus she started cursing at him. And then she actually drove off in her car.

The next day, she came back to HEX and the boss said, "You have to take criticism unless you want to get fired."

She said, "I'm not exactly the kind of person who accepts criticism immediately." And so then she was fired.

When Baquisha lost her job, she went off to the ghetto life. For instance she actually had a saying: *Chitty chitty bang bang, bitches gonna die.* She lost her house because she didn't pay the rent, and she didn't want to live there anymore because she wasn't paying her bills. And because she wasn't paying her bills, her kids were raunchy—they hadn't taken a shower in weeks and she couldn't afford to buy them new drawers or new shirts or no new pants or nothin'. They couldn't even flush the toilet when they used the bathroom. The house smelled terrible. So getting kicked out actually put them in a better environment. At least the outside world didn't smell bad.

✹

But let's back up a bit, back before the kids and the stink and all the giving up. This was back when Baquisha just had her one little man, Rude Boy, and she was still doing what she could to lead a good life.

One day Baquisha was dragging her child along the street on the way to Giant. She was looking back talking to her son when she ran into a man.

"Baquisha, is that you?"

"Who the heck are you? And why are you talking to me?"

He said, "It's me, Chris."

"I know a lot of people, but I don't know a Chris."

"You really don't remember me, from childhood, and high school? We had a child together!" As he said that her little boy, RB, and Baquisha looked at each other with one eyebrow up and a smirk on their mouths.

"No really," he said. "We had a child together. His name is Rude Boy. Because when he came into this world he always hit me and always loved you."

She said, "Oh right. I remember that. I had a child named Rude Boy with a man named Chris... but he walked out on us as soon as RB was born. He just left the hospital when he saw his baby's face. And when I ran after him, he said, 'I'm not ready, I can't do this. You have to raise him on your own.' And I said, 'Fine, OK, just don't ever come back.'"

RB said, "Mom, is all this true?"

Chris put his hand on RB's head and his other hand on his own heart and said, "Yes, all of this is true. But I still love you as my child."

Baquisha covered RB's ears and she said in a smart tone, "Why are you just bringing this up now?"

"What do you mean?" he said.

"I know who you are, fool, I just want no part of you. As I said at the hospital: Do not come back, do not act like you are

10

part of this family."

"Come on now. As long as we known each other... why you gotta be like this?"

"Well, I'm sorry if I do not want my son traumatized after seeing his father for the first time in his life and thinking that I'm such a lousy mother that I could never bring him to see you."

"Well, I'm sorry for being such a lousy father. I just couldn't handle the pressure when I first saw the little boy's face."

"Well, still. You could have at least told me instead of just walking out on me when I didn't even know."

"I SAID I WAS SORRY. WHAT MORE DO YOU WANT FROM ME?"

"What I wanted from you was for you to actually stand up and be a good father, and I'm not saying you had to be perfect, no, I'm just saying all I asked for was for you to at least take care of your child *some of the time.*"

"Mommy, are you okay?" said RB.

"Yes, baby," she said. "Mommy's just having some issues. Stuff you'll understand when you're older if you ever have to go through this." She looked back at Chris with a sly face. He reached out for her. She shook her head, but she reached back.

The next day, he moved in.

Nine months later, they had twins. One name was obvious: Rude Girl. The other was Tianna.

Now, as the years passed, Baquisha wasn't exactly the best influence on her kids. Trinitoga did that to her. Being with Chris, who was then called Shoota, the King of the Hood, that did that to her, too. Every time her kids were asking for something, she was too busy. She was selling drugs. She was using drugs. And what might be the best way to put it? Well,

photo by Jonae Haynesworth

"What I wanted from you
was for you to actually
STAND UP
and be a good father,
and I'm not saying
you had to be
perfect."

she was just being a bad influence.

Her three kids—RB, RG, and Tianna—were really mad when they were growing up because of how she acted towards them. Since their mom acted extremely bad towards them, they forgot how to do many things. When they enrolled themselves in school, they had troubles just like their mom did.

They also had troubles because when they went to sleep they would dream about their mother dying because of her drug addiction, or they dreamed that someone would kill her because of all the money she had to give to people for supplies for the drugs.

One day their dreams almost came true. Baquisha was in their old stanky alley, which was where they lived since they got put out of their building, and she was drug dealing. She told the person that she owed the money to—her boss—that she didn't have it on her. So her boss made her flinch like he was gonna shoot her. Then she thought he might shoot her for real.

Baquisha started to run. She ran into a different alley and saw that it was a dead end.

Her boss decided that for his last words to her, he was gonna use her line: *Chitty chitty bang bang, bitches gonna die.*

And when he said that, Baquisha said, "I love my family, and I wish they had a better life." She put her hand over her heart and she praised the Lord. Then he shot her in her heart.

Somebody heard the shooting and they called the ambulance. They rushed Baquisha to the hospital and then to surgery. She was in pain, although they had given her many pain medicines and many other things, but nothing worked.

Eventually, Baquisha's heart stopped and the heart monitor went off and the doctors even put the cover over her face. But then a miracle happened—as soon as the doctors and nurses walked out, they heard a heartbeat on the heart monitor. Beep. Beep. Beep.

13

When Baquisha was dead for those moments, she had flashbacks of her childhood and how her mother treated her. One image was Baquisha's mother beating her after she had helped her grandmother, but at that time, her mother thought she was hurting her grandmother. Baquisha didn't have any time to explain herself. Her grandmother tried to explain, too, but her mother didn't care. She just beat Baquisha anyway.

Another image was how Baquisha's mother and grandmother had made Baquisha sleep outside on the porch because she had spilled the rice out of the pot when they cooked a feast for Thanksgiving. When she was sleeping outside, some dogs attacked her, and her mother didn't care. She said, "That's what you get, Baquisha, for being so bad." And Baquisha said to herself, "Lord, what did I ever do, that my mother and grandmother treat me like this?"

When Baquisha came back to life, she jumped up and started breathing heavy. The memories made her feel like they were real again. When she was breathing, she wondered where she was and how she got there and what happened to her.

The doctors said that she had almost died. The bullet had stopped at the edge of her rib.

What saved her was the fact that her hand was over her heart.

by Reiyanna Davis

14

Sharkisha

Sharkisha was 18 years old and lived in this very bad hood called Trinitoga. If you went there, you might be a little scared. There were rats running everywhere, and drug addicts and homeless people sitting on corners. She had lived there since she was four years old, and she loved it. It was her home. It was her childhood and her hometown, and so she was going to fight for it.

Sharkisha was so bad, when you saw her, you ran. They even made a song for her: "Cock your hand back and hit it like a nisha BOW!" If you even looked at her the wrong way or mugged at her, it would be a big problem. Her favorite saying was, "Take a picture, it would last longer," and if you really did it, she would knock you out and break your phone.

Sharkisha was having a bad problem, though. Her mom was trying to put her out because the opps kept knocking on the door every day. So Sharkisha was staying with her boyfriend, Rude Boy, until further notice. Everywhere she went, she tried to duck from the opps.

One day on her way to the store Sharkisha saw her mother with some dude. She looked at her mother, looked at the dude, and called out, "I can't believe you have another dude." She was about to go off on her. Her mom kept bringing different dudes to the house so she didn't pay any attention to Sharkisha.

Sharkisha was getting fed up.

Her mom said, "How am I going to feed you without any man in our lives?"

Sharkisha then felt some type of way. She felt sad on the inside and angry on the outside. So without thinking first, she slapped her mother.

Her mom tried to swing, but Sharkisha stopped it by catching her hand.

Somebody in the background started singing Sharkisha's favorite song and Sharkisha punched her mom in the face. She felt stupid because her mom fell on the floor. Her mom had a bloody nose and her eyes were closed. Even though she and her mom didn't have a good relationship, she still didn't try to intentionally hurt her.

She looked at her mother for about two seconds and then heard the siren. She started to run.

The police pulled up saying, "Stop, you stupid dog."

Sharkisha kept running, and she ran into her boyfriend RB. They ducked into an alley and the cops ran by. Sharkisha caught her breath, but then she told RB what happened. She was worried about her mom. She was like, "I gotta go to the Trinitoga Clinic," and he said he'd meet her after.

When Sharkisha got to the Clinic, she went to the room that the lady at the front desk told her to go to, but her mom wasn't there. So then she went up and down the hallways looking in each room for her mother. No luck. Finally she saw her mother and the doctor walking down the hallway. She ran to them. Her mother stared at her.

"Doctor Chichi, can you get me a bottle of water?" her mother said to her.

photo by Jahmes Hamilton

Sharkisha felt
some type of way.
she felt s a d
on the inside
and ANGRY
on the outside.

"What? No, Mommy, this is Sharkisha."

"Who's Sharkisha?"

"Me! Your daughter!"

"I never had kids. What are you talking about?"

Then her mother pushed away from her. The doctor said she had amnesia from the hard hit. He asked her, "Do you know who did this to her?"

Sharkisha was feeling sad, because she never should have hit her mother. Pain, hurt. Regret. "No," she said. And then she ran out of there.

Sharkisha ran back to Trinitoga and told her boyfriend RB everything that happened at the clinic, and while she was talking she was talking very fast.

He yelled, "Shut up and get a hold of yourself."

"Don't tell me shut up, you shut up!" she yelled back. How could he treat her like this when she needed him? She didn't want to be with him so she ran off again, this time to her house. She got there and realized that she didn't have the key. Sharkisha just sat on the steps for hours thinking of how her whole entire day went. She couldn't believe it.

At some point she gave up and went to sleep outside. It was extremely hot. She kept flipping.

Eventually someone tapped her awake. A voice said, "Why are you sleeping outside?" It was RB. He said, "Come on. Get off that dirty ground and come to my house."

Sharkisha sighed. "I'm still mad at you," she said. "But OK. I have nowhere else to go."

The next morning she went up to the hospital and when her mom saw her, she said, "Sharkisha, Sharkisha, is that you?"

Sharkisha said, "Yes, Mom, it's me." She was surprised and happy because her mom was with her now and she didn't have to be lonely anymore. She said, "Mom, I'm so sorry for what I did to you."

Her mom said, "What are you talking about? I don't remember you doing anything wrong."

Sharkisha said, "Mom, I'm telling you the truth. I put you in this position that you're in."

Her mom shook her head and said quietly, "I know what happened and why I'm here, but I'll forgive you for now. I just want to go home. Just you and me."

Sharkisha nodded. That was all she wanted, too.

When her mom got inside and saw the house she said, "This place looks like a trash dump. What happened to this rathole?"

Sharkisha remembered letting all that anger out the other night, throwing stuff. "There was a tornado," she said, and when her mom looked confused she just laughed and said, "I'll clean it up. You just go in the room and rest."

Sharkisha was feeling better. She felt like that was a low point and it wasn't going to get lower. She tried calling RB to tell him about it, but he didn't answer. A few minutes later she got a text from him that said:

```
going 2 hospital. my mom
```

Again? Sharksiha thought. RB's mom was always drama. She felt grateful her own mom was safe and asleep in the other room. They had problems, yeah, but everyone had problems. For now, at least, they were doing OK. They were living on.

✵ by Temil Whipple

rude girl

It's the morning of yet another day of school, and Rude Girl's mom is downstairs drinking energy drink mixed with coke and Cîroc. Rude Girl is upstairs getting ready, but she feels a little cranky, because she feels like she has to go to school with negative energy on her—because of her mom. She's brushing her hair, finding socks. She's an unorganized person, and her room is junky. Everything is everywhere.

She gets to school and feels sad because all she keeps thinking about is her mom's addiction. Last year her mom almost died when she was shot over a fight about drugs and since then she said she'd change. But she hasn't changed. Rude Girl begins to cry, not noticing that her classmates are wondering why and looking at her. She looks up and feels like her whole life is just worth nothing.

After first period her teacher tells her to stay behind so that she can have a talk with her. Rude Girl already knows what this is about. Her teacher asks her little questions like, "What's wrong? Would you like to share your news with me? You can tell me anything. So...?"

Rude Girl says she does not want to talk. She keeps moving without answering her teacher's questions.

That evening when Rude Girl gets home, her teacher calls her mom and tells her that Rude Girl has been sad. Her mom gets really upset and starts to drink. Great.

Rude Girl gets to thinking, *What would my life be like if I was not with my mom?* She starts packing a bag. Her mom walks in but Rude Girl doesn't notice at first and her mom says something unclear. Then her mom falls down and Rude Girl gets scared.

"MOM, ARE YOU OKAY?"

Not a word comes from her mom.

Rude Girl knows what to do. She gets on the phone and calls an ambulance. She tells the operator her mom's problem. She says, "Hurry, hurry, quick! Apartment 6, Edgewood Street NE. My mom has passed out from her addiction to drugs."

"OK, OK, we will try to be there as fast as possible."

Two minutes later, Rude Girl hears the ambulance. She is crying next to her mother, and when the ambulance pulls up, the paramedics are in such a hurry that they actually push her. She goes ape when she gets pushed, like a gorilla. And then, after that, she tries to run after the ambulance, but the police stop her. Four men. They say that she has to go separately. Her friend Stacy and her mom had come out when they heard the sirens, so they tell her, "We'll take you."

The hospital looks big on the outside, but on the inside it is narrow. She remembers this, from when she was here just last year, when her mother was shot. She can't believe she's back here again.

It is quiet while they wait for the doctor to come give them the news. Her mother is on a breathing machine. The doctor comes to them. He has glasses and is chubby. His eyes are indented. He says, "We're sorry to give you the bad news, but your mom is not doing so well. We don't think she's going to make it."

Rude Girl gets up in his face. She starts cursing, saying, "You mean to tell me that my mother is hopeless, and you didn't do a thing? You doctors didn't do shit to save her life?"

The doctor says, "We're really sorry. We tried our best."

Rude Girl says, "Shut up and take me to my mother." She shakes him and smacks him and even spits on him. She does everything. Rude Girl brings out her talent for acting out so she can see her mom. She commands the doctor to take her to her mom's bedside, and he does what she asks.

When she goes into the room with Stacy and Stacy's mom there is a moment of silence. Rude Girl touches her mother's face. She says, "No no no no no no, why you gotta, why you gotta go? No no no no no no, God just let her stay home. Just let her stay home."

Everyone else leaves the room, so Rude Girl is alone with her mom. She doesn't know what to do. She sits on her mom's bed and can see that everything has gone wrong, just by looking at her mom's heart monitor.

She says, "Mom, if you were able to hear me right now you would say sorry, but it's too late. I know it is. I'm sorry I let this happen to you. It's all my fault. It's all my fault."

But then something changes inside her. She slaps her mom and says, "You know what? This ain't my fault. You said you were going to change. I told you to stop, and now you have to pay your own price." And then the doctor runs in and Rude Girl gets put out of the room.

"Get the hell off me. Dis her own damn fault. I told her, I told her..." And then Rude Girl drops down and starts crying. "I'm sorry. I just don't..."

She has no words. She has no hope.

Fifteen minutes later, Rude Girl finds out that her mother is dead.

She walks right out of the hospital. She'll come back, eventually, when her father shows up, and then her brother and her sister, and she'll grieve together with all of them. But right at that moment when she first hears her mother is gone, she just walks right out. She does not know where else to go. She does not know what else to do.

26

photo by Jahmes H

"Mom,
if you were able to hear me right now
you would say sorry,
but it's too late.
I know it is.
I'm sorry I let this happen to you.
It's all my fault.
It's all my fault."

Two weeks later they have the funeral but they don't have enough money to bury her, so they burn her. After it is all over, Rude Girl goes alone and dumps her mom's ashes into the sea. She does not think twice. She doesn't have feelings for her mom because of the way her mom treated her. That treatment makes her the way she is. She isn't like this with everyone, just with her mom.

Five years later, Rude Girl is twenty-one and she is about to have a baby and get married to a man named Marquis. Rude Girl has changed over time. She has a job. She's grown up. She still thinks about her mom even though she had problems with her. Most of all, Rude Girl loves her man and will do anything for him.

"Marquis, Baby, come down here. I need you to get something for me."

"Coming, Baby." Marquis comes downstairs to help his woman get some crackers out of the cabinet. She is eight months pregnant. They both go upstairs and watch TV. Rude Girl falls asleep next to him.

Marquis leaves the house and goes to get his other daughter, Nana. Rude Girl knows about Nana—she is thirteen years old. Marquis is not with his daughter's mom.

So when Rude Girl wakes up, he isn't there. She feels like something isn't right. She calls him because she is worried.

"I'm not feeling well," she says. "I think it might be the baby."

Marquis comes to get her and takes her to the hospital. He is feeling fine, he isn't worried. He has already been through all of this because he had one other kid. Rude Girl is not so sure.

When they get to the hospital, everything happens fast. The doctors give Rude Girl medicine so she won't feel the pain. Five pushes later, she gives birth. The baby is a girl. They decide at the hospital to name her Gabriella. She is a pretty baby, but she is premature. She is two pounds, five ounces. They get to visit her every day, twice a day.

A month later, Gabriella comes home. At this point, she is ten pounds. She is healthy. She sleeps all the time.

Marquis and Rude Girl smile and laugh and never leave the baby out of their sight. They play with her. They are in the bedroom while Gabriella is sleeping.

Rude Girl thinks a lot about her own mother, and the way she treated her. She doesn't want to treat Gabriella that way. She says to Marquis, "I'm going to be a better mom than my mom was."

Marquis says, "I know you are."

✴ by Zoe Williams

tianna

I came home late after school and did not see Mom or Rude Girl. There were beer bottles on the table and there was beer all over the kitchen floor. I wondered where my mom was. I figured she went for a walk, like she usually does when she's mad.

I started to go look for her when India, who is my best friend, came running down the street. "Tianna," she said. She was out of breath. "Your mom is at the hospital. They took her like an hour ago."

"What?" I said. I started to panic.

"But it's going to be all right," India said. "You should come to my house. Rude Girl is up there with her, and so is your father."

"They're with her?" I said. I wanted to go to the hospital so bad, but I also wanted to go to India's, where I could pretend it wasn't happening. Since my father was at the hospital, I thought maybe everything was OK. Maybe this terrible feeling in my stomach was wrong.

"Tianna, I have this cool book I think you should read," she said. I could tell she was trying to get my mind off things.

"Okay," I said. "I will read it." But I knew I wouldn't be able to.

✻

When we got to India's house, her phone started to ring. I

knew that it was the doctor from the hospital and I knew what he was going to say. India answered.

"Yes this is her," she said.

A pause.

"Okay, I will tell her, thank you," India said as she started to hang up the phone.

I said, "Who was that?"

India looked more serious than I've ever seen her look before. "Well, it was the doctor. They said that your m..."

Before India could even say "mom" I busted into tears. I ran out the door without saying anything. I ran to the playground where my mom used to take me and Rude Girl when we were young. I thought at least that going to the playground I would think that my mom was still with me. I was imagining the scene of me and Rude Girl with our pretty curly hair and our mom pushing us on the swing and us laughing and just having fun.

Suddenly I heard footsteps. I saw someone with all black on, and a long beard. He had a gun in his hand. I said, "Please, I don't have anything for you."

He said, "You do. You have my money."

I said, "I don't have any money. What are you talking about?"

He walked closer, and lifted the gun up and said, "Stop playing, Rude Girl, and give me my money. You owe me, like, ten grand."

"What are you talking about? I am not Rude Girl. Rude Girl is at the hospital."

"Stop lying all of the time. What are you, her twin or something?"

"Yes, I am, actually." He lifted his gun up and pointed it at me.

I started to run.

He said, "Come back here!" And then he started to chase

I ran to the playground
where my mom
used to take me
when I was young.
I thought at least
that going to the playground
I would think that my mom was
still with me.

me.

So I ran as fast as I could to the police station.

He ran right into the police station and pulled his gun out and said, "Rude Girl, give me my money now!"

All the police pulled their guns out and said, "Drop your weapon."

He didn't drop it. He started shooting. I was breathing hard. This was craziness. I ran to the back and hid under a desk. When I heard, "Hold your fire!" I jumped out from behind the desk and said, "I'm not Rude Girl!" as loud as I could.

The guy had killed a cop. He was lying there on the floor, bleeding. I stared at him and couldn't believe it.

The next thing I knew, I was in handcuffs. They put me in a room and started asking me questions. "What happened? How old are you?"

I said, "Look, check the cameras! Check the cameras!" I was sitting there crying. "Look," I said. "My mom just died." I could barely speak. "I ran because I was upset, and this man held a gun to me, and I didn't know what to do. I'm only 16." I shook my head, trying to clear it. "After you check the cameras from the playground on Haynesworth Street, then I will answer all your questions."

✹

Eventually they believed me. They started calling numbers to get someone to pick me up. Rude Boy answered and said, "Hello?"

The people at the station said, "This is MPD Police and we're calling about your little sister, Tianna. You need to get here quickly."

He said, "OK. I'm on my way."

So then he got to the police station and he saw me in

handcuffs, and he said, "Oh lord, what did she do? Or what did I do?"

"I didn't do anything!" I said.

"What happened then? Why are you in handcuffs?"

"I was at the playground where Mom used to take us," I explained. "Then this man walked up to me with a gun and said, Rude Girl, you owe me ten grand."

That's when Rude Boy said, "Oh no! That's JJ from the block. I know him. We used to be homeboys. Rude Girl does owe him a lot of money."

I said, "Well JJ is dead because he started a shootout at the police station because he thought I was our sister." Then I said, more quietly, "And Mom is dead, too."

He gave me a look like, *Are you kidding, or are you serious?*

"I'm serious." I looked away. "Call Rude Girl and ask her."

Rude Boy dropped to his knees. He started crying. I don't know that I'd ever seen him cry before.

The policeman saw what was happening and let me out of the handcuffs. I hugged my brother. We didn't really get along, but in this moment we needed love.

He wiped his face and said, "What hospital is Mom at? We gotta go up there."

"She's at Fine Point Hospital."

That policeman was still watching us, and now he looked like he actually cared. He stood up. "Do you need an escort?" he asked.

"Yes, anything that can get us to the hospital," Rude Boy said.

As we were getting into the car, we saw that somebody was getting robbed across the street and we told the policeman. But he ignored it because he heard no screams, no gunshots, no nothing. In Trinitoga, without that, it didn't count.

While we were riding in the car, my eyes started getting watery and I started sniffling. Rude Boy was texting somebody—Sharkisha, probably, he was always texting his nasty girlfriend—but he stopped when he heard me crying. He put his arm around me and said, "Come on, Tianna, give me a hug." I started to lean against him but I faked it. I started freaking out in the car.

"She only started drinking and smoking when you and Rude Girl started stressing her out. Yelling at her, not coming home, stealing her money."

He slapped me. He said, "What is wrong with you? Get some sense in your head. See, you're acting just like Mom when she's drunk. It's her own fault. It's her own fault she died. Always getting drunk and high."

I started to ball my fist up and my face was turning red. I'm a really nice girl but when people say stuff about my mother I get really offended. So I started hitting him back.

"Pull the car over!" he yelled. "My sister is freaking out back here."

The police said, "What are you guys doing back there? Stop kicking my chair. Quit fighting. We're pulling up at the hospital now."

Rude Boy said, "Stop it, we're here."

I jumped out of the car and ran into the hospital. I yelled, "Baquisha White! Where is my mother?" to the nurse sitting at the desk.

The nurse said, "Calm down. Your mother is in Room 215, straight down the hall to your right."

Rude Boy said, "Wait up, wait for me."

I didn't stop. I kept running until I got to the room. I dropped to my knees. I saw my mother lying in the bed with her arms across her chest and Rude Girl sitting in a chair rocking from side to side. Our dad was walking back and forth.

I was feeling chest pains, panicking.

Then Rude Girl got up and hugged me. Rude Boy started crying again and Rude Girl hugged him, too. It was the closest the three of us had been in years. Normally I wanted nothing to do with them, I only wanted out, but at that moment we were all that we had.

That's when the nurses came to move the body.

Rude Girl said, "No. Where are you taking my mother? She's staying here." I watched her and could tell by the way she was crying and her shoulders were slouched down that she felt like she should have shown our mom better respect.

The doctors said, "Okay, we'll leave you with her for five minutes, and then we have to take her so that her body won't start to smell."

They left her body in the room. Rude Boy and Dad walked out. They couldn't handle it any more. Then it was just me, and Rude Girl, and Mom.

Rude Girl went to Mom's body and kissed her on her forehead. She said, "Mom, I'm sorry I never gave you the respect you deserved. I remember what you used to say, that you never realize how much you love someone until they're gone and now I realize how much I miss you. I'm going to change and not hang in the streets or stay out late smoking and drinking." She gave our mother one more kiss.

I watched in silence. I couldn't think about my own future right then, but I wondered about my sister's. Would she make empty promises like our mother? Or would she really change?

As with all the hardest things, we would have to wait and see.

✷ by Jonae Haynesworth

As with
all the
hardest things...

03/07/2014 PM 05:23

photo by Zoe Williams

india

This is a story about me, India. I am 16 years old and live in Renwood with my grandma. I have a best friend named Tianna who lives in a bad hood called Trinitoga. Tianna has a twin sister named Rude Girl, who I don't like because she is mean and she always picks on little kids, but she won't fight anyone her own size. She fights like every day because somebody looks at her the wrong way, or somebody accidentally bumps into her. She is like a bully, and I'm nice. Until you push me to a certain point.

Tianna and I were talking on the phone about how Tianna doesn't like her family. They're not very good people.

"Oh my god," Tianna said.

"What?" I said.

"Guess what just happened."

"Your father just shot somebody?"

"No!"

"Then what happened?"

"My muva is mad at me, Bruh."

"What did you do? And I'm not your Bruh."

"I ain't do nothing, Bruh."

"Stop lying, and stop calling me Bruh. I'm not Bruh!"

"BRUHHHH!!!!"

Anyway, Tianna was talking about people dying on the day before her mother died. That night her mother was smoking bad things. The house was really, really nasty and trifling. They had trash and clothes and ashtrays and everything on the floor. It was dark because they didn't pay their electric bill. They didn't have hot water because they didn't pay the gas bill. They were about to get evicted, because they didn't pay their rent.

"I hate it here," she said.

So Tianna came over to my house. We got tired of talking about her family and their drama, so instead we talked about boys, people we liked. The boys we were talking about were Daquan, Sean, Marcus, and Chris -- not Shoota Chris, but the boy-with-the-thick-eyebrows Chris. Shoota was Tianna's father and she really didn't like him. He was a thug. She used to love her father, but not anymore. Now he only looked after his own self, and he got mad at Tianna for going over to my house. He thought she thought she was too good for him or something.

Anyway, the other boys... Daquan was freaky. Girls be running from him. Sean was just funny. Too funny. Marcus was gonna get kicked in the face, but he was funny, too. Chris— thick eyebrows Chris! He did the same sign in every picture. Like a rock star sign, because he thought he was awesome. He thought he was Shyglizzy.

Then we started talking about Sharkisha and said she was a THOT. A THOT meant "That Ho Over There." She was Tianna's older brother Rude Boy's girlfriend. Sharkisha took after her mother, following in her mother's footsteps. She found out that she was made on a one-night-stand, and wasn't supposed to be born. When Sharkisha found that out, she started sleeping with different people, and she caught AIDS. RB didn't know that she had AIDS, and we thought that was not cool. If her brother catches AIDS, Tianna told me, she's gonna beat the crap out of Sharkisha.

The next day we went to school as usual. Rude Girl seemed to be in a bad mood all day, but what else was new. Tianna had something to do after school so I told her I'd see her later.

When I got home, Rude Girl called looking for Tianna. "She's not here," I said. Rude Girl sounded sad and worried. "Our mother just had a heart attack," she said. I gasped.

"Is she OK?" I asked.

Rude Girl didn't answer.

"Just tell Tianna when you see her," she said. "But tell her she doesn't have to come to the hospital. Not yet. I'm here. Dad's here. We'll call if something happens."

"OK," I said. I hung up. I didn't have a good feeling about this. But I needed to keep Tianna calm. I ran to her house as fast as I could to try to catch her.

You already know what happened next. I found Tianna outside her house, looking for her mom, and I told her what happened. I did what Rude Girl said and told her not to go to the hospital. I tried to keep her from worrying. She seemed both upset and angry. On the walk to my house she was like, "I don't want to go anyway."

"Why not?" I said. "I mean, it's your mother." I never knew my own mother, because she died when I was still a baby.

"I don't want to go, because I already know why she had the attack, and I wanted her to stop smoking, but she didn't." She folded her arms over her chest and looked away, but I could tell she was wondering what would happen.

And then we got home and the doctor called. Rude Girl gave him my number. She told him that Tianna should hear it from me.

But I couldn't even say it.

I started to, but my face gave it away before I could finish. I said, "They said that your m..."

And then she just ran out the door.

"Your mother died," I said to the empty room.

Her mother was dead.

I couldn't believe it, but I could, too. I felt both at the same time.

I was worried. What was going to happen to Tianna? Would she just start acting crazy and mean like her sister now that her mother was dead?

❋

Grandma and I looked for Tianna for a long time after she ran off but we couldn't find her. We went to the hospital hoping we would find her there, and we did. Everyone was there. Tianna and Rude Girl and Rude Boy were all just standing around, kind of in shock. The nurses had just taken away their mother's body and the family was trying to figure out what to do. Tianna said they were grown, and now they could all go their separate ways. She wanted to get out of there. They went outside into the alley, and I went with them.

Her father was there, too. He looked like he always looked, because him and his wife never really got along. But he looked upset, too, because it was the mother of his children who died. He started screaming at people. He looked at Tianna standing with me and said, "You not gonna keep going over there. You're gonna come home."

"No, I'm not," she said. "I'm staying with India."

I was just standing there, listening and watching them argue. I was nervous because I knew that Shoota was crazy and he just might try to kill his own daughter.

Shoota looked at his kids and said, "Y'all ain't splitting up, ya'll are staying together. Nobody's going nowhere."

"No," Tianna said again. "I'm going with India."

"You ain't goin' nowhere," Shoota said.

"Yes she is, she's coming with me," I said.

So then that's when Shoota said to me, "Little girl, who are you talking to?"

"I'm talkin' to you," I said. I was proud of myself for sticking up for my friend and for myself. But I was also nervous. I knew how crazy Shoota was.

"You're not about to tell me where my daughter can and cannot go."

"Yes I am. She's not going with you. She's coming back with me."

And then he pulled up his shirt, put his hand on his hip, and took out a gun and shot me.

Chitty chitty bang bang.

I dropped.

I felt pain and was shocked that he actually shot me.

The bullet hit me in the arm and I could see blood.

Tianna started cussing out her father, asking why would he shoot the only person she really liked in this world.

"You have a smart mouth and you shouldn't be hanging with her."

"Since when do you care who I hang with?"

"Since your mother died, and life is too short."

While they were having this argument, I was lying on the ground, bleeding to death, and my grandmother was calling 911.

42

My grandmother was screaming.

I was feeling pain. I was in pain. I was almost unconscious and I wasn't saying anything. Everybody thought I was dead. He shot me in the arm. The bullet stopped in my arm.

People from the hospital ran out, and the police came and locked Shoota up.

And then I was in a coma.

While I was in the coma, angels came and visited me. They told me it wasn't my time to go. The angels were my mother and father, who had died in a car crash years ago. I felt so happy to see them. I felt happier than I'd felt in so long.

Two days later, I woke up. Over those two days, Tianna stayed with me. Her mother was too ghetto to have a funeral. They just lit candles and carried them around where she died. Tianna didn't even go to that.

"What happened?" I said when I woke up. She told me later that I looked dead. I was pale. My lips were cracking, and my skin was dry, and I looked like I needed some lotion.

Tianna said, "Long story short, I hate to break it to you, but you got shot. By my father."

"Huh? Why was your father shooting me?"

"Because you said to him that you could tell him where I could go."

"Well," I said. "Too bad for him."

Tianna smiled. "Let's get you out of here. Let's go home."

by Trinity Alston

43

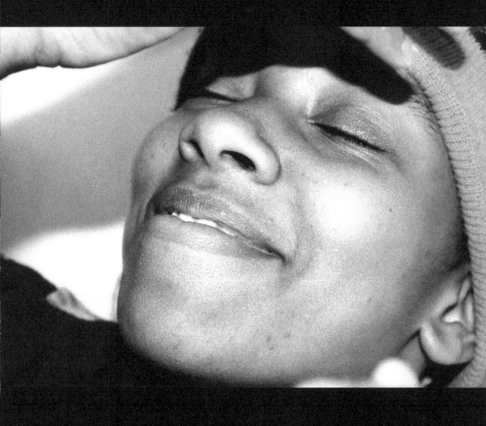

While I was in the coma,
angels came
and visited me.
They told me it wasn't my time to go.
I felt so happy to see them.
I felt happier than I'd felt
in so long.

India's epilogue

I bet you want to know what happened after that. I can't tell you everything, but I can tell you some. First of all, Shoota ended up in jail for life. Besides shooting me, he had so many counts against him: selling weed, robbery, killing. He was a lost cause, but it's too bad, because I heard that at some point he was actually nice. A good kid with a bad life. That's what happens, I guess.

His son Rude Boy followed in his footsteps and ended up in jail, too. At least for a few years. Tianna finally told him she heard that Sharkisha had AIDS, and he got in big fights about it, trying to defend her honor. It turned out it wasn't true. Lots of things you hear turn out that way. But Sharkisha moved away not long afterwards anyway, all the way to Jamaica, where her father lived. I heard that she actually turned out OK, became a nurse or something, took care of her mother. But Rude Boy, he stayed bad. He got in even more trouble after she left, like now he had no reason to even try to be good.

Rude Girl, believe it or not, she changed her life around. She became a mother. A great mother. She got married to a really sweet man. We see them all together, playing with their little girl, Gabriella. She's a totally different person now. Calm and kind. But she still goes by Rude Girl. Some things just do not change.

And me and Tianna? We got a house together, and we live together still. Tianna had a baby named Henniya and I became an aunty. I love being an aunty, and I am so glad we are still such good friends.

So that's where we are now. We're in a good place. We came a long way, growing up in Trinitoga. We have a long life still left to go.

✹ by the Editors

45

acknowledgments

This book could not have been possible without the support of a number of hard-working folks who believed in the importance of empowering these young people to write and share their stories.

For the striking photography throughout the book we thank Shout Mouse Photo Coach and Shootback founder Lana Wong. Lana brought her considerable artistic talent to these writers and coached them to create the beautiful images we see here. We are grateful for her dedication and her vision.

We are also grateful for the talents of Shout Mouse Story Coaches Elizabeth Gutting and Alison Klein, both of whom played crucial roles in developing these stories and inspiring these writers. Elizabeth led the workshop charge for much of the drafting process and became a terrific mentor to these authors. She also drew the map of Trinitoga! Alison joined the workshop in those all-important last few weeks and helped these writers finish and polish their stories. Both coaches assisted in book editing, as did Story Intern Sarah Cooke, who spent countless hours doing layout, copyediting, and offering smart editorial insight. For this support and so much else, we are so grateful!

For coordinating the writers and encouraging them on so many fronts we thank the tremendous staff of Beacon House, and in particular, Gerry Stevens-Kittner, Nandi Turner, and Reverend "Rev" Robinson. We are so happy to partner with Beacon House for this project. We hope that this book demonstrates the crucial role that the organization plays in the lives of these young people, providing a safe and enriching space for them both to develop necessary skills and to dream big dreams.

None of this work would have been possible without an introduction and generous grant from the HMFC fund, for which we are so thankful.

And most of all we thank the dedicated writers who spent their spring Friday afternoons thinking hard, laughing hard, and putting hard and heartfelt stories on the page. The creativity and the insight of these authors will stay with us. We are so proud. We are excited for them, and we are moved. We are already ready for their next book!

about the authors

Trinity

Hi, my name is **Trinity Alston**. I'm 11 years old. I go to John Burroughs. I like to play softball and cheerlead. My favorite color is pink. Writing this story was a way of telling people what is going on in my life without people knowing some things are really me.

Reiyanna

My name is **Reiyanna Davis** and I'm from Washington, DC. I enjoy many things, like sports, swimming, and cooking for the family. Some things I like to cook are grilled cheese, chicken nuggets, French fries, and occasionally breakfast. I also like to play with my friends. When I grow up I want to help the needy and work in the entertainment business. This story has been an adventure of sadness, love, and happiness. Also a little drama.

about the authors

Jonae

My name is **Jonae Haynesworth** and I am a 13-year-old eighth grader writing this book from Beacon House, which is located in Washington, DC. I used to play sports like basketball and soccer and run track, and now I play softball and football. I like to write books with drama and action.

serenity

Hi, my name is **Serenity Summers**. I'm 11 years old. My favorite color is purple. I go to DC Prep EMC. I have always lived in DC. Writing this story was fun because the story sounded like it was real.

about the authors

Temil

My name is **Temil Whipple**. I am a 12-year-old seventh grader and I like to write fantasy, mysteries, and action stories. I used to run track, do cheerleading, and play basketball, and now I play softball and football. I like shoes and clothes and technology. And I'm smart.

Zoe

Hi, my name is **Zoe Williams**. I like to cheer, sing, and play football, basketball, and softball. I'm a wonderful person in many different ways. My favorite color is purple and I go to DC Prep and have lived in Washington, DC since Day 1. I am in the sixth grade and am 11 years old but will be 12 in two months. My favorite artists are Beyoncé and Tray Songs and Usher. I love them because they make good music.

about beacon house

Beacon House is a non-profit, community-based organization that provides tutoring, mentoring, cultural, athletic, recreational, and nutritional programs to at-risk children, ages 5-18, who reside in and around the Edgewood Terrace community in Ward 5 of Washington, DC. Our mission is to assist at-risk youth to identify and pursue educational objectives that culminate in college or vocational training, and, more generally, to prepare them for productive involvement in their community and society. Beacon House's goal is to lift as many children as possible up and out of their often difficult circumstances.

Beacon House was founded in 1991 by Rev. Donald E. Robinson in response to an overwhelming need for social service programs for youth in what was once a drug and violence-plagued community. Over the years, Beacon House has grown into a professionally-run organization and operates out of two 6,000 square foot spaces within the Edgewood Terrace apartment complex with nine full-time and more than a dozen part-time staff who, in turn, manage dozens of volunteers, partnerships with complementary not-for-profit programs, and an array of programs that nurture hundreds of children a year. While most of the youth reside in and around the Edgewood Terrace neighborhood in Washington, DC, no one is turned away.

Beacon House is funded by individuals, foundations, local and state governments, and corporate donations and grants.

beacon**house**
Where Learning Has A Home

www.BeaconHouseDC.org

about shootback

Shootback empowers young people to tell their own stories and express their creative voices through photography, writing, and critical thinking about the world around them. Shootback started in Nairobi, Kenya in 1997 by putting cameras in the hands of teens from Mathare, one of Africa's largest slums, and culminated in the publication of *Shootback: Photos by Kids from the Nairobi Slums*, a documentary film, and an international traveling exhibition. Seventeen years on, Shootback continues to train a new generation of young photographers and now runs after-school programming in DC public schools in collaboration with City Year DC.

Shout Mouse Press is proud to partner with the Shootback team, who coach our authors to produce striking original photography for our books.

SHOOTBACK   www.ShootBackProject.org

about shout mouse press

Shout Mouse Press is a writing program and publishing house for unheard voices. We partner with other nonprofit organizations serving communities in need and design custom book projects that benefit their communities. Our mission is two-fold:

- To amplify the voices of marginalized communities by empowering them to write and publish their stories.
- To amplify the missions of the nonprofits with whom we partner by creating tangible, marketable products that diversify and innovate their outreach and fundraising.

Shout Mouse Press was founded in Washington, DC in 2014. Our authors have produced original children's books, memoir collections, and novels-in-stories that engage readers of all literacy levels, ages, and backgrounds. See our full catalog of books on our website.

SHOUT**MOUSE**
PRESS

www.ShoutMousePress.org

We Believe

We believe everyone has a story to tell. We believe everyone has the ability to tell it. We believe by listening to the stories we tell each other—whether true or imagined, of hopes or heartbreaks or fantasies or fears—we are learning empathy, diplomacy, reflection, and grace. We believe we need to see ourselves in the stories we are surrounded by. We believe this is especially true for those who are made to believe that their stories do not matter: the poor or the sick or the marginalized or the battered. We feel lucky to be able to help unearth these stories, and we are passionate about sharing these unheard voices with the world.

SHOUT**MOUSE**
PRESS

CPSIA information can be obtained
at www.ICGtesting.com
Printed in the USA
LVHW07s1540050418
572434LV00026B/340/P